Anonymous

Manual of the Church of the Pilgrimage

Anatiposi

Anonymous

Manual of the Church of the Pilgrimage

Reprint of the original.

1st Edition 2023 | ISBN: 978-3-38211-154-0

Anatiposi Verlag is an imprint of Outlook Verlagsgesellschaft mbH.

Verlag (Publisher): Outlook Verlag GmbH, Zeilweg 44, 60439 Frankfurt, Deutschland
Vertretungsberechtigt (Authorized to represent): E. Roepke, Zeilweg 44, 60439 Frankfurt, Deutschland
Druck (Print): Books on Demand GmbH, In de Tarpen 42, 22848 Norderstedt, Deutschland

MANUAL

OF THE

CHURCH OF THE PILGRIMAGE,

PLYMOUTH, MASS.

1870.

Jesus Christ himself being the chief corner-stone.
EPH. ii. 20.

CAMBRIDGE:
WELCH, BIGELOW, AND COMPANY,
UNIVERSITY PRESS.
1871.

HISTORY.

THOU SHALT REMEMBER ALL THE WAY WHICH THE LORD THY GOD LED THEE. — Moses.

WE locate the beginning of the history of this church, in respect to time, near the close of the sixteenth and the first part of the seventeenth centuries ; and, in respect to place, across the sea, in England.

The principles of the Reformation had for a long time, by reason largely of the circulation of Tyndale's translation of the Bible, attracted general attention throughout England, and had become deeply fixed in the minds of many of the people ; and Henry VIII., who reigned from 1509 to 1547, had gained to himself the title of "Defender of the Faith" for his zeal in opposing them. But on account of the refusal of the Pope to divorce him from Katharine, his wife, he summarily, in 1534, divorced that part of the Catholic Church included within his rule from its allegiance to Rome, and established a regal in place of a papal supremacy in religious and ecclesiastical matters. He made himself Pope in England in place of Clement VII.

With this single change, the Church continued for a considerable time very much as before. But in order to conciliate, on the one hand, those who still adhered to the Church of Rome, and on the other, those who avowed the Protestant faith, it assumed, under the reign of Edward VI. (1547 – 1553), a character of compromise between the excessive rites and ceremonies of the Papal worship, and the extreme simplicity of worship of the Reformed churches. During the five years of Mary's reign it was set back to its original allegiance to Rome, and many were driven from the realm by persecution ; while many, among whom were Ridley, Latimer, and other prominent preachers of the Reformed faith, suffered death by martyrdom. On the accession, however, of Elizabeth, the yoke of Romish tyranny and intolerance was finally cast off; an act of supremacy was passed, declaring her to be the head of the Church, which was soon followed by the "Act of Uniformity," requiring all religious worship to be conducted according to the model of the State, and by the adoption of the Articles of Religion. Thus came into permanent being the Established Church of England.

Very soon and very naturally the different elements combined in this constitution of the Church began to develop themselves in strife and division. We see the germ of this difference in the refusal of John Hooper, in 1550, to take the oath of supremacy until King Edward had erased a part of it; and note the evidences of its gradual growth in the separate congregations of exiles established at Frankfort, Zurich, Geneva, and other places, during Mary's reign, many of whom returned when Elizabeth came to the throne; in a similar movement in England in 1566; in the proposal of Cartwright, four years later, to reduce all things relating to church government to the apostolic method of the New Testament. The Church thus resolved itself into two parties, — Prelatists and Puritans; the former being earnestly desirous to continue the resemblances to Romanism which lingered in it, while the Puritans, contemptuously so called, desired to have every vestige of them removed. They acted as a reforming party within the Church, to which, as a body, they continued loyal, firmly believing in a union of Church and State, or in the right of the State to hold supremacy in religious matters. They thought that by the power of the State the Church should be still further reformed. For this they labored, for this they suffered. Throughout the entire reign of Elizabeth (1558 – 1603) they were opposed and persecuted, were fined, imprisoned, deprived of their goods. Nor was their case improved as they had hoped, but rather made worse, in the succession of James.

But in connection with the continuous failure of the Puritans to effect the changes which they desired, a tendency began to appear, in more and more evident forms, to question the authority itself of a State Church. There were some who, as Bradford says, "began to see farther into these things by the light of God's Word"; to see that the "lordly and tyrannous power of the prelates was contrary to the gospel, and that their authority to load men's consciences ought not to be submitted to." Many began to deny openly the right of the State to direct and control the religious methods of its subjects, and to affirm, in place of this, the right of every man to worship God according to the dictates of his own conscience and his personal understanding of the Holy Scriptures. In 1582 the doctrine was advanced by Robert Brown, that, according to the New Testament, any body of Christian men, associating themselves together by a willing covenant, was a church, and, as such, had power to govern itself, independently of all external control. In accordance with these views, large numbers, feeling that they could not conscientiously continue in the Established Church, renounced their connection with it and became known as Separatists. Churches were formed in different places upon the self-governing idea. The movement provoked a bitterness of persecution unknown within the period ; and some — as Barrow, Greenwood, and Penry in 1593 — suffered martyrdom for their loyalty to the principles of Congregational Church government.

It thus appears that the Puritans and the Separatists were two entirely different parties. Although Puritanism may have been the germ of which Separation became the flower, — although the position of Separatists may have been reached through the Puritan way, — there was yet a vast deal of Puritanism that never came to the flower ; there were a great many Puritans who never became Separatists. As adherents in principle to the English Church, the former settled in 1630 in the Bay of Massachusetts.

The origin of the Church of the Pilgrimage at Plymouth is found in one of the principal congregations in which this movement crystallized ; in that which was formed at Scrooby, Nottinghamshire County, in the North of England, as early as 1602. Prominent among those composing it were Richard Clyfton, John Robinson, and other ministers in that and the adjacent counties ; also William Bradford, of the neighboring village of Austerfield, and William Brewster. The place in which they were accustomed to meet was a large manor-house occupied by Brewster, then postmaster at Scrooby, and an earnest advocate of the principles of Separation. They formed in 1606 "the church which was in his house," when, in Bradford's words, they "joyned themselves (by a covenant of the Lord) into a church estate, in ye fellowship of ye gospell to walke in all His wayes, made known, or to be made known unto them, according to their best endeavours, whatsoever it should cost them, the Lord assisting them." This was the beginning of the Mayflower Church.

They soon found that, on account of the fearful and increasing persecution to which they were subjected on every side, it would be impossible for them to maintain themselves in England. They found that King James meant to be true to his purpose to " harry them out of the land," unless they returned to the church they had left. They therefore, with much regret for the necessity, and much opposition and delay in the process of removal, sought refuge in Holland, where they had heard "was freedome of Religion for all men." After remaining in Amsterdam about a year, they removed to Leyden. John Robinson was formally settled as their pastor ; William Brewster was chosen ruling elder. They were joined while here, by John Carver, Robert Cushman, Edward

Winslow, and others, from England. Here they continued "a church by themselves"; "enjoying," as Bradford has said, "much sweet and delightful society and much spiritual comfort together in the ways of God," and "lived together in peace and love and holiness." Their relations were also pleasant with those around them, and the influence of the exile church was strongly felt for good.

Their abode here, however, gradually wrought within them the conviction that Holland could not make for them a suitable permanent home. They found it to be a country in which it was extremely difficult to obtain comfortable support; that many among them were suffering on this account, while many for the same reason were kept from joining them. They were also deeply exercised for the welfare of their children, whom, owing to the peculiar temptations of a manufacturing city, they found it difficult to train in thorough Christian ways; while they wished to preserve and perpetuate their distinctive English name and tongue. The noble thought, moreover, found place within them, that, by removing, they might lay "some good foundation" for advancing the Redeemer's kingdom in other parts of the world. At length, having continued in Leyden eleven or twelve years, the thought of removal became for these reasons their settled purpose; and almost concurrently with the growth and formation of this purpose, they were led to choose the "vast and unpeopled countries of America," then under the dominion of the king of England, as the place of their future home.

Accepting the memorably "hard terms" by which the

relations of the enterprise to the English government were finally adjusted, it was agreed among themselves that the younger and stronger portion of the church should go at first; also, that those who went should offer themselves freely; and that, if the larger part went, Mr. Robinson should go with them ; if not, the elder, Mr. Brewster, only. As the result of this arrangement the number of those who volunteered to go was slightly less than half. The pastor therefore remained, and, as they were about to leave Leyden for Delfthaven, fourteen miles distant, preached to them a memorable sermon from Ezra viii. 21, and, just before leaving Delfthaven, knelt upon the shore and "comended them with most fervente praiers to the Lord and his blessing." After repeated reverses and delays, this pioneer Pilgrim company left Plymouth, England, September 16, 1620, in number one hundred and two persons, and ended an ocean voyage of much anxiety and peril by anchoring, November 21, in the harbor of Provincetown. On the 16th of December a third exploring party went forth, and after searching along the shore two or three days, came to "Clark's Island," where, in the words of the record, "On the Sabbath day we rested," and on the following Monday, December 21, 1620, landed on Plymouth Rock.

It had been the earnest, assured hope of the Pilgrims that their beloved pastor, with others whom they had left in Holland, would soon join them. But through deceptive dealing on the part of some of the merchant adventurers, who had furnished money for the enterprise, and had become jealous of its religious character, he was kept year

after year from doing so, until, in March, 1625, he was
taken to his rest above. Meanwhile William Brewster
ministered acceptably to the church in all things except
the sacraments, of which, during this period, it was, with
much grief, deprived. We are told that " many were
brought to God by his ministry" ; and from the beginning
the religious life of the colony was a radiant fact ; " the
church in the wilderness," though depleted by the death
of many of its members, among whom was Carver, one
of its deacons, continued to live. Regular Sabbath services were held ; probably during the first year in " the
common house "; subsequently in the lower part of the fort
erected early in 1622, east of the Cushman monument, on
Burial Hill.   On the 10th of November, 1621, a vessel arrived from England bringing thirty-five persons, one of
whom was Robert Cushman, who, shortly before his return
a month later, preached a sermon on "The Sin and Danger
of Self-love," from 1 Corinthians x. 24.   It was the first
sermon preached in New England.   On the 11th of December the Pilgrims kept the first Thanksgiving, "our har-
vest being gotten in."   The first fast was observed in July,
1623, on the occasion of a severe, long-continued drought.
Near the end of the same month the colony was again
reinforced by the arrival of two ships from London, with
sixty passengers.

In 1624 a man by the name of Lyford was sent over by
those who had prevented Mr. Robinson's coming, to act
in the interest, secretly, of Episcopacy, as pastor of the
church.   But his treacherous designs were soon discov-
ered, with other immoralities, and he was expelled from

the colony. In 1628 another man by the name of Rogers was sent over to be the minister of the church, but was likewise refused. In the following year the church extended a call to Rev. Ralph Smith, just arrived at Salem, who was duly installed as the first successor of John Robinson. He continued in the office five or six years, and during the last three years of his ministry was assisted by the celebrated Roger Williams. New arrivals took place in this and the following year from the church in Leyden. In 1632 the first church that went out from the church at Plymouth was formed at Duxbury; and shortly after, in the same year, another was organized from it, — the first church at Marshfield. Two years later the church at Scituate was formed by a reunion of several members of the Plymouth church with about thirty members from the church at Southwark, London, with whom they had been associated before leaving England. It was about this time that Archbishop Laud and others of the Established Church made an attempt, upon authority of Charles I., to deprive the colony of all the rights which had been granted it, and replace its existing form of government, both civil and ecclesiastical, with another, of such kind as to them might seem expedient. Had this attempt succeeded, the church at Plymouth would doubtless have been destroyed, and the colony reduced to abject bondage. But its success was happily prevented by the timely efforts of Edward Winslow, the agent for the colony, then in England. In 1636 Mr. John Reyner, "an able and godly man," became the third pastor of the Mayflower Church, with whom, from 1638 to 1641, Rev.

Charles Chauncy was associated as an assistant. In the year 1637, one of the colony gave by will "somewhat" to " Plymouth meeting-house." A building, probably the first church edifice of the Pilgrims, was subsequently erected, the site of which is suggested by an ancient deed, which speaks of the north side of Town Square as "the spot where the old meeting-house stood." The church was deeply afflicted, in 1644, by the death of William Brewster, who was succeeded in the office of ruling elder by Thomas Cushman. About this time its members were led to consider seriously the question of giving up the settlement at Plymouth on account of its unpromising condition, and a majority at length determined upon removal to Eastham, on Cape Cod. The project was, however, afterward abandoned ; but some who were intent upon going thither were dismissed and organized into a Congregational church in that place. "Thus was this poor church," as the records say, " left like an ancient mother grown old, and forsaken of her children, though not in their affections, yet in regard of their bodily presence and personal helpfulness ; her ancient members being most of them worn away by death, and those of later times being like children translated into other families, and she like a widow left alone to trust in God. Thus she that had made many rich became herself poor."

In addition to these trials, the church became involved soon after in a long-continued "first encounter" with religious error, which appeared throughout New England in the form of Quaker and Antinomian teachings. Its prosperity was also weakened by a sentiment embraced by some of its members, of opposition to an educated and salaried ministry, which, more than anything else, caused the withdrawal, in 1654, of Mr. Reyner, and, with the exception of occasional supply, kept them destitute of a pastor fifteen years. Its purity was at the same time sadly compromised by its adoption, with most of the other New England churches, of the decision of the Synod of 1662, called the Half-way Covenant, which allowed unregenerate persons to be received into membership with the church. In 1657 another of its most valued and useful members, William Bradford, was removed by death. In June, 1669, Rev. John Cotton, son of the celebrated John Cotton of Boston, was installed as the fourth pastor, and continued in the office thirty years. The low estate of the church at this time is indicated by the fact that it contained but forty-seven resident members. As a bright and cheering feature, however, amid so much that was dark and depressing, it is pleasant to notice the extent to which the Pilgrims had already been the means of " advancing the gospel of the kingdom of Christ," as indicated in the large number of " praying Indians" in the settle ments at this period, and in the existence of several Indian churches ; also in the fact that a complete translation of the Bible had been made into the Indian tongue. The second edition of this Bible was corrected by Mr. Cotton, who sometimes preached to the Indians in their own language. In the year 1683 a new house of worship was erected at the head of Town Square. We note in 1685 the death of Nathaniel Morton, author of the New England Memorial, and also of the records of the church from its beginning to 1667 ; and in 1691, the death of Thomas Cushman, the ruling elder, to which office Thomas Faunce was chosen after some years.   In 1694 a church was formed at Middleboro' by a union of several members from Plymouth with others from other places ; and two or three years later, a similar procedure resulted in the formation of the church at Plympton, then a part of Plymouth. Mr. Cotton was succeeded in 1697 by Rev. Ephraim Little, the fifth in the occupancy of this office, in which he continued until his death, in 1723.   He was the first minister buried in the Plymouth burying-ground.   We have a record of temporal reverse in the partial destruction in 1715, by lightning, of the meeting-house.   In 1717 several members of the parent church were organized into a church in the north part of the town, now Kingston.   In July of the year following the death of Mr. Little, Rev. Nathaniel Leonard was installed as his successor, and continued in the office thirty-two years.   In 1734 a union of some of the Plymouth members with others from Middleboro' formed the church in Halifax ; and November 8, 1737, twenty-five members of the original church were organized into the Second Church in Plymouth, at Manomet Ponds.

We reach here the period of the " Great Awakening " under Edwards and Whitefield, in which the church at Plymouth participated, and by which, owing to the sad influence of the Half-way Covenant, and the Arminian tendencies of some of its members, it was brought to a decisive test with respect to its purity and doctrinal soundness.   Many were offended ; a violent opposition to the emphasis given to the leading doctrines of evangelical religion, especially that of regeneration, arose, and resulted in a withdrawal, in 1744, of some of the members of the church and society, and their organization into the "Third Church and Congregation" of Plymouth, by whom a house of worship was built on King, now Middle, street. "The society was never large, though comprising much of the wealth and fashion of the town." It continued in existence until 1776, when, having become greatly reduced in number, it was dissolved by mutual consent, and, not long after, the meeting-house was demolished, and the members of both church and society returned to their former connection. In July, of 1744, the first society built a new house of worship on the same spot occupied by the former. Nearly two years later occurred the death of Thomas Faunce, the last ruling elder of the church. About this time, and again in 1754, we read that Whitefield visited Plymouth and preached with great power and acceptance to crowded audiences.

Mr. Leonard continued pastor of the church till 1756, when, owing to physical infirmities, he asked and received a dismission, and, in 1760, was succeeded by Rev. Chandler Robbins, D. D., whose pastorate continued until his death in 1799, and was characterized by faithful, kindly intercourse with his people, and by thorough evangelical teaching. About four or five years before his death, the same spirit which had once withdrawn from, and returned to, the church, began again to show its unrest in the proposal of about fifty persons in the parish, not relishing the distinctive doctrines of Christianity, to be released from their connection with it for the purpose of forming a new society. Their proposal, however, not being granted by a majority, was withdrawn ; and largely out of personal regard for Dr. Robbins, they continued to bear their proportional part in the support of worship. But when, by reason of his death, it became necessary to obtain another pastor, the desire for a more "liberal" style of preaching, which meanwhile had been dormant but not dead, reasserted itself with renewed earnestness in the church and society, and resulted in the choice of Rev. James Kendall to the pastoral office, who was installed on the first day of January, 1800.

There were those, however, who from the first had refused to concur in this result ; and the ministry thus begun had continued somewhat more than a year, when a goodly number, not satisfied with the modified form in which the doctrines of the gospel were presented, and determined to remain true to the faith of their fathers, began to feel that they could not, consistently with their views of religious duty, continue longer in the original church. This conviction deepened rapidly into a settled purpose, and, on the first day of October, 1801, fifty-two persons, eighteen males and thirty-four females, but one less than half the entire number, withdrew, and organized themselves as the Third Congregational Church of Plymouth ; and on March 30, 1802, one hundred and fifty-four persons were incorporated into the Third Congregational Society of Plymouth ; declaring, in their petition for incorporation, that they "could not longer conscientiously unite in public worship with those from whom they had separated."

This movement involved no small degree of sacrifice on

the part of those by whom it was made, not only of feeling and outward inclination, but also of the temporal appliances of worship; inasmuch as the church edifice, the ground on which it stood, the funds devoted to the maintenance of worship in it, the records which told the story of the religious life it represented, were sacred to evangelical sentiment and doctrine. But all was left, our later, like our earlier ancestors, choosing rather to abandon things like these than to compromise their loyalty to the faith delivered unto them. It was a repetition in miniature of the original act of separation which initiated the Pilgrim history; and, in singular coincidence with the precedent of that history, is said to have been the first of many similar movements which took place in the State, during the first part of the present century.

From the period of this division, the first church of Plymouth has been a Unitarian church, and it is with the new organization that the remainder of our history has to do.

A house of worship was built on the westerly side of "Training Green"; and, on the 12th of May, 1802, Rev. Adoniram Judson was installed as the pastor, the eighth in the succession from John Robinson; and continued in this position until 1817, when, by reason of his adoption of Baptist views, the relation was dissolved. During this period the blessing of God rested evidently upon the church; believers to the number of about ninety were by letter and profession added to it, and, in 1813, a church was formed chiefly from its membership at Chiltonville, under the name of the Fourth Congregational Church of

Plymouth. Mr. Judson was succeeded by Rev. William T. Torrey, whose pastorate continued about five years. In 1824 Rev. Frederic Freeman became the pastor. Two or three years later the meeting-house was enlarged and remodelled. In 1830 a spirit of division and dissatisfaction with respect to the existing ministry, which had been manifest for some time, culminated in the withdrawal of about fifty members of the Third church and the formation of the " Robinson Church," or the Fifth Congregational Church of Plymouth, by whom a house of worship was erected on Pleasant street. Three years after, Mr. Freeman closed his labors and was succeeded by Rev. Thomas Boutelle, who held the pastoral office until April, 1837. Rev. Robert B. Hall was installed in the August following.

On the 24th of November, 1840, a new house of worship, which has since been occupied by the society, was dedicated with appropriate services under the name of "The Church of the Pilgrimage." Its dimensions are sixty-eight feet by fifty-nine, with a tower twenty-six feet square. It stands very near, if not directly upon, the site of the first church erected by our Pilgrim Fathers (see page 16), and received its name in commemoration of their pilgrimage to this place. A view of this church is given in the engraving (see Frontispiece), on the right of which is seen a portion of the chapel dedicated March 3, 1852 ; also, rising directly from its base, a section of Burial Hill, where the remains of many of the Pilgrims rest.

A new society, called the Society of the Pilgrimage, was organized shortly after the dedication of the church.

Mr. Hall continued his ministry until the spring of 1844, when, by reason of his "preferences for the doctrine, discipline, and worship of the Protestant Episcopal Church," it was brought to an end. In May, of the year following, Rev. Charles S. Porter was installed as the pastor. During his ministry the Robinson church disbanded ; and at the communion of October 19, 1851, fifty years from the first communion service of the Third church, a large number of its members were received again into fellowship with this church, and others continued subsequently to come. The house in which they had worshipped was sold to, and is still occupied by, the Methodist society. Mr. Porter closed his pastorate February 1, 1854, and was succeeded by Rev. Joseph B. Johnson, who was installed on the 4th of January following, and continued the pastor two years. In September, 1857, Rev. Nathaniel B. Blanchard, who had supplied the pulpit for a short time previous, was invited by the church and society to become their minister, and continued to act in this capacity, though not installed, until the summer of 1860. The church remained destitute of a regular ministry from that time until the autumn of 1861, when Rev. P. C. Headley assumed the supply of the pulpit, and continued his labors through the winter and spring, though declining the invitation given him to become the settled pastor. Rev. W. W. Woodworth "entered into" his labors and continued to act as stated supply to the end of March, 1864. In November of this year Rev. David Bremner was installed as the pastor, and held the relation until August, 1868. During the interval of transient supply which followed, the house of worship was repaired and made to assume its present condition of convenience and comfort. The present pastor was installed on the 13th of April, 1870.

By a vote of the church on the 5th of May last, its name was changed from that of the "Third Church of Christ in Plymouth," under which it was organized in 1801, to that of "The Church of the Pilgrimage," and was thus made to conform not only to the name by which for a long time it had been currently known, but also to that of the society organized in 1840, and to that by which the new edifice was the same year dedicated ; so that the present name of these two organizations is, "The Church and Society of the Pilgrimage, Plymouth, Mass."

Such is an outline of the outward history of this church from its beginning to the present time. But let it not be thought, as we have thus traced it, that it is the history of a mere externality. These visible, successive facts are but the expression of an inward life. Their essential, evolving principle has, we believe, been that of an indwelling Christ. This is evidenced by the fact that, notwithstanding the adverse events which have so often gathered about it from without, and the restless tendencies repeatedly developed from within, it has continued to live and grow. It has shown a power to preserve and perpetuate itself, to eliminate error, and maintain and advance the doctrine of Christ. It has been refreshing, in looking through the records of the church, to find frequent instances of a renewal of covenant on the part of its members, and to note its occasional observance of days of humiliation, fasting, and prayer, and of thanksgiving for special mercies. While the repeated revival scenes to which we have come have been like the wells and palms of Elim to the Israelites ; the more recent of which are gratefully remembered by many now. Nor has it merely kept itself in being, but has, as we have seen, thrown off numerous coruscations of its life, which have become bright lights in other places. According to the history given, ten churches have, either wholly or in part, been formed from it.

This is but a statement in subjective terms of the kindly, preserving care of God for his Church and for his gospel. To Him be all the glory.

We recognize the Church of the Pilgrimage to be identical, in all essential respects, with the church of Scrooby, Leyden, and of the early wilderness of America ; and apply to it the words of Morton, at the close of his Introduction to Bradford's History : " The Church of Christ at Plymouth in New England, first begun in Old England, and carried on in Holland and at Plymouth aforesaid." It is thus the first and oldest church of America. The church at Scrooby, from which it came, was organized ten years before the Congregational church at Southwark, London, from which mainly the church of Scituate, the larger part of which afterward removed to Barnstable, was formed. Although its organization changed in 1801, the same long current of previous life continued, and is still resident in this church. As the identity of an individual is not changed by a legislative change of name, neither does a change of the organization, which is but the outward form or name for the essential, interior life, affect necessarily the identity of a church. We believe that an impartial, comprehensive eye, tracing through the years the line of ecclesiastical history over which our view has passed, would, on reaching the beginning of the present century, make the turn which we have made, and see that history perpetuated in the Church of the Pilgrimage of to-day.

It is the same in doctrinal faith, which is the vital, preserving secret of identity, and from which the essential character of a church is formed. By the necessary condition of a oneness of doctrine, its members are constituted "the direct spiritual heirs and successors of the Mayflower Church." We may still say, in the words of John Robinson : "Our faith is not negative." "Our faith is founded upon the writings of the Prophets and Apostles." Its creed affirms "the same great truths of 'the glorious gospel of the blessed God,' to maintain which our fathers fled to these Western shores, under the influence of which they lived, in the belief and love of which they died, and 'which they left it in solemn charge to their posterity to maintain, whatever temporal sacrifices it might require, to the end of the world.'" Its present Articles of Faith, with the Covenant and Rules of Government, were adopted November 28, 1870. (See pages 32 – 44.)

During the incipient days of the Scrooby congregation, the Rev. John Smyth, pastor of a Separatist church formed by him at Gainsborough, in the neighboring county of Lincolnshire, in 1602, and the venerable Richard Clyfton, whose labors were much blessed in its advancement, seem to have been associated in its pastoral care. On the removal of the former with his people to Amsterdam, in

1604, Clyfton assumed the entire ministerial charge, in which, soon after, he was assisted by John Robinson, to whom it was at length entirely transferred. The church, although organized in 1606, does not seem to have become thoroughly settled in its organization until the removal to Leyden, when Robinson was chosen and installed as pastor. It is quite evident that he was the first who was formally installed in this office. We therefore place his name at the head of the list of pastors of this church. (See page 45.)

The office of the ruling elder seems to have combined some of the duties belonging to that of the pastor and the deacon, holding a midway place between the one and the other. (See Dexter's Congregationalism.) It ended with the death of its third incumbent, in 1746, being justly regarded as no longer necessary or desirable. (See page 46.)

The church, while remaining entire in Holland, " had three able men for deacons." The name of one of them, who probably remained there, with the time also of their choice, is unknown. It is quite probable, however, that they were chosen about the same time Brewster was chosen elder, and we have therefore given this date. Nor is the record fully definite with regard to the time of choice of the fourth, fifth, and ninth in this office, but associates it, more nearly than with any other, respectively with the years given. The choice of the sixteenth and seventeenth in the list is located in the spring of 1716 ; hence we have placed it in April. The record makes no mention of the choice of the twenty-ninth, and we therefore place it in the first year during which he is spoken of as deacon. It also gives the year only of the choice of the thirty-fourth and thirty-fifth, but leads us to infer that it was not earlier than September. (See pages 46, 47.)

The total number of members of this church, by whom the long line of succession we have followed has been maintained, cannot be given with absolute certainty. Before the departure of the Mayflower Pilgrims the church at Leyden numbered about three hundred. Regarding the greater part of those who came over, subsequently to the first arrival, as already members, we have no record of additions until the beginning of Mr. Cotton's ministry, in 1669, during which there were added one hundred and seventy-eight persons. During the ministry of Mr. Little one hundred and fifty-nine additions are recorded ; during that of Mr. Leonard, three hundred and thirteen ; from the beginning of Dr. Robbins' ministry to the division in 1801, two hundred and twenty ; from the division in 1801 to the present time, seven hundred, — making a total, according to these numbers, of one thousand eight hundred and seventy persons. The only record which we have, with respect to the number received during the first fifty years, from 1620 to 1670, is that, at the beginning of Mr. Cotton's ministry, there were forty-seven resident members. Adding to this a fair proportion of absent members, and, at the same time, making all due allowance for those of the entire number who may have remained of the Leyden membership, it seems but reasonable to suppose that the number received additionally, during this interim, would make the total membership of this church from the beginning not less than two thousand, while

probably it would make it more, — a number which, dis-
tributed in spaces of less than a year apart, would form a
continuous line to the time when Christ was on the earth.

From the date of the new organization, in 1801, to the
present time, the entire number constituting the membership of this church consists of the fifty-two original members, and of seven hundred since added, — in all of seven
hundred and fifty-two persons ; five hundred and eight
having joined by profession, two hundred and forty-four by
letter. Of these, two hundred and thirty-one have been
removed by death, and two hundred and thirty-one by dismission to other churches. The total present membership
consists of two hundred and fifty-five persons ; and, as
a complete register of members from the first cannot be
given, it has been thought best to give simply a list of
those composing this number. (See pages 48 – 55.)

But " our fathers, where are they ? " As we think of the
great proportion of those constituting the entire membership of this church, who, we doubt not, are resting now
from their pilgrimage and rejoicing in the glory of the
heavenly world, we cannot fail to be impressed with our
nearness to eternal scenes. The line of history, which we
found to begin at the village of Scrooby, seems to begin no
longer there, but to stretch down, in diagonal course, from
the City of God. The thither end of it has been lifted.
God has reached down and caught it up and fastened
it about his throne. The life of earth has been trans-
figured into the life of heaven. Robinson and Brewster, Smith, Cotton, and Robbins, Judson, Porter, and
Blanchard, and all the earlier ministers and members of

3 *

this church, are there. The descending line draws nearer
to us as we think of those who have more lately died.
Its hither end is fastened about ourselves. We are in
close and vital connection with those who, during the history of this church, have ascended from its membership to
glory, — members of the same body, possessors of the
same " goodly heritage," lovers of the same Christ.

> " One family, we dwell in Him, —
> One church above, beneath."

We would, in closing this review, make thankful record
of the fact that the present condition of the church is one
of peace and prosperity. The services of the sanctuary
are well attended ; the meetings for social religious worship are well sustained. A Sabbath school is in success-
ful operation. The various processes of church life are
in healthful, harmonious exercise. The blessing of God
in temporal and in spiritual things is abundantly manifest.

May the future of the Church of the Pilgrimage be ever
worthy of its past. May it be in days to come what its
members in days of old were pleased to call it, " an in-
closed garden," in which " the righteous shall flourish like
the palm-tree," and the fruits of grace shall be richly mul-
tiplied, and out of which every false, unhealthful growth
shall be carefully kept. May the mantle of Elijah rest
upon Elisha, its present and future members maintaining
in all purity " the faith once delivered unto the saints " ;
taking up this radiant line of former years and making it
longer, brighter still ; transmitting from generation to generation, even to the end of time, the grand succession.

" Wherefore, seeing we also are compassed about with so great a cloud of witnesses, let us lay aside every weight, and the sin which doth so easily beset *us*, and let us run with patience the race that is set before us,

"Looking unto Jesus, the author and finisher of *our* faith."

"Now unto him that is able to do exceeding abundantly above all that we ask or think, according to the power that worketh in us,

"Unto him *be* glory in the church by Christ Jesus throughout all ages, world without end.   Amen."

ARTICLES OF FAITH.

(See page 26.)

I. WE believe in the existence of a personal God ; and in the Scriptures of the Old and New Testaments, as a record, given by inspiration of God, of a revelation of himself to man, and the only perfect rule of our faith and practice.

1 Tim. ii. 5. Jer. x. 10. Isa. lv. 9. Matt. vi. 10. 1 John iv. 19.
2 Tim. iii. 16. 2 Pet. i. 21. John v. 39 ; xvii. 17. Heb. i. 1, 2.
Ps. xix. 7, 8 ; cxix 105.

II. We believe that there is a Trinity of persons in the Godhead, — the Father, the Son, and the Holy Spirit ; and that these three are one God, the same in substance, and equal in every divine perfection.

Matt. xxviii. 19. 2 Cor. xiii. 14.
Exo. iii. 14. Ps. xc. 2. Matt. v. 48. 1 Kings viii. 27. Mal. iii. 6.
Rom. xi. 33. Jer. xxxii. 17. Dan. iv. 35. Exo. xxxiv. 6, 7. Rom.
i. 25.
Isa. ix. 6 John i. 1 – 18 ; v. 16 – 32. 1 Tim. iii. 16. 1 John v. 20.
Micah v. 2. Col. ii. 9. Matt. xxviii. 20. Heb. xiii. 8. John x. 18 ;
xxi. 17. Heb. i. 3, 8. Rom. ix. 5.
Mark xii. 36. Acts v. 3, 4. Heb. ix. 14. Ps. cxxxix. 7 –10.
1 Cor. ii. 10, 11 ; xii. 11. Rom. xv. 19. Eph. iv. 30.
Deut. vi. 4. John xiv. 7 – 10 ; xv. 26. 1 Cor. viii. 4. 2 Cor. iii. 17.

III. We believe that God has an eternal purpose to declare his own glory as the chief end of all his works; and that, according to this purpose, he created, preserves, and governs the universe.

Gen. i. 1, 2. Job. xxxiii. 4. Col. i. 16. Neh. ix. 6. Heb. i. 3. 1 Chron. xxix. 11.

Isa. xiv. 24 – 27. Acts ii. 23. Rom. viii. 28 – 30; ix. 15 – 24. Eph. i. 4 – 11; iii. 11.

Prov. xvi. 4. Isa. xliii. 7. Rom. xi. 36. Rev. iv. 11. 1 Cor. x. 31.

IV. We believe that God created man in his own image, and gave him a law requiring holiness, and sanctioned by the penalty of eternal death upon the transgressor; that, in the beginning, man was holy, but fell from that estate by disobedience; that, in consequence, men are by nature destitute of holiness and prone to sin, justly exposed to God's displeasure, and unable to deliver themselves " from the body of this death."

Gen. i. 26, 27; ii. 16, 17. Eze. xviii. 4. Rom. vi 23.

Gen. i. 31. Eccl. vii. 29. Gen. iii. 6 – 8, 16 – 19, 23, 24.

Gen. vi. 5. Ps. xiv. 2, 3. Rom. iii. 9 – 19, 23; v. 12 – 21; ii. 8, 9. Eph. ii. 3. Rom. vii. 24. John xv. 5.

V. We believe that God, in the second person of the Trinity, became incarnate in Jesus Christ, and has, by his humiliation, sufferings, and death, made an atonement for sin, sufficient for the whole world; that, since the depraved condition of the heart is such, that none will turn to Christ except the Father draw them, the Holy Spirit comes to reprove the world of sin, of righteousness, and of judgment; and that regeneration by the influence of the Holy Spirit is essential to salvation.

> Matt. i. 23. Luke i. 35. John i. 14. Gal. iv. 4. Heb. ii. 14 – 17. Isa. liii. Matt. i. 21 ; xxvi. 28. Acts iv. 12. Rom. iii. 24, 25. 1 Cor. xv. 3. 1 Tim. i. 15. 1 Pet. ii. 24.
> John iii. 16. 1 Cor. viii. 11. 1 Tim. ii. 6 ; iv. 10. 1 John ii. 2.
> John v. 40, 42 ; vi. 44, 65. Rom. viii. 7, 8. 1 Cor. xii. 3. John xvi. 8 – 11. Acts ii. 2 – 4.
> John i. 12, 13 ; iii. 3, 5 – 7. Rom. viii. 9, 10. 2 Cor. v. 17. Eph. ii. 1. Titus iii. 5. Rev. xxi. 27.

VI. We believe that faith in the Lord Jesus Christ is the great condition on which men may be justified and saved ; that all who will may thus receive the water of life freely ; and that those who, through faith, are renewed by the Holy Spirit, will finally attain to everlasting life.

> Mark xvi. 16. Acts xiii. 39 ; xvi. 31. Eph. ii. 8. Ps. xxxi. 19. Matt. xiv. 30. Rom. iii. 20 – 28 ; x. 9 – 11. James ii. 20 – 24.
> Isa. lv. 1. Matt. xi. 28. Rev. xxii. 17.
> Ps. xxxvii. 24. Prov. iv. 18. John v. 24 ; vi. 39 ; x. 28, 29. Phil. i. 6. 1 Pet. i. 5. 1 John ii. 19.

VII. We believe that the Christian Sabbath is of Divine appointment and authority ; also that the Lord Jesus Christ has a Church in the world, to which all regenerate persons should belong ; that the Sacraments of the Church are Baptism and the Lord's Supper ; that the proper recipients of baptism are the infant children of professing Christians, and believers on profession of their faith not before baptized ; and of the Lord's Supper those only who are in good standing in the Church.

Gen. ii. 3. Exo. xx. 8 – 11. Mark xvi. 2, 9. John xx. 19. Acts xx. 7. 1 Cor. xvi. 2. Rev. i. 10.

Gen. xii. 1 – 3. Acts vii. 38 ; xx. 28. Matt. xvi. 18. Eph. i. 22, 23 ; iii. 21. Matt. x. 32. Acts ii. 47. 1 Cor. i. 2. 2 Cor. vi. 17. Titus iii. 10.

Matt. xxviii. 19. Acts ii. 38. Matt. xxvi. 26 – 30. 1 Cor. xi. 23 – 26.

Gen. xvii. 7 – 10 ; xviii. 19. Deut. vi. 7. Luke xviii. 15, 16. Acts ii. 39 ; xvi. 15, 33 ; xviii. 8. Rom. iv. 11 ; xi. 17 – 24. 1 Cor. i. 16 ; vii. 14. Gal. iii. 14 – 17.

Acts ii. 41 ; viii. 37 ; ix. 18 ; x. 47, 48.

Luke xxii. 19. 1 Cor. v. 7, 8 ; x. 16, 21, 31 ; xi. 27 – 29.

VIII. We believe that all men, irrespectively of character, are immortal, and do, at death, enter upon their respective rewards of glory or of misery; that Christ will come again at the end of time, to raise the dead and judge the world ; and that the wicked will at that day "go away into everlasting punishment," and the righteous be received into everlasting life.

Gen. i. 27 ; v. 24. 2 Kings ii. 11. Job xix. 26, 27. Isa. xiv. 9. Matt. x. 28; xiii. 47 – 50. Luke xx. 38 ; xvi. 19 – 31 ; xxiii. 43. Phil. i. 21 – 23. Rev. ii. 10 ; xxii. 11.

Matt. xvi. 27. Acts i. 11. 1 Thess. iv. 16. Luke xxiv. 6. 1 Cor. xv. Matt. xxvii. 52, 53. John v. 28, 29. Matt. xxv. 31 – 46. 2 Cor. v. 10. Rev. xx. 11 – 13.

Isa. iii. 11. Matt. xii. 31, 32 ; xxv. 41 – 46. Mark ix. 43 – 48. 2 Thess. i. 7 – 9. Heb. x. 26 – 31. Jude 6, 13. Rev. xxi. 27.

Ps lxxiii. 24 ; Matt. xxv. 21, 34. John xiv. 3 ; xvii. 24. 2 Pet. i. 11. Rev. vii. 9 – 17.

Do you thus believe ?

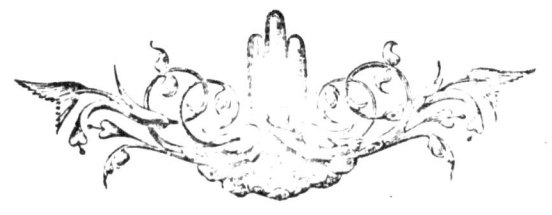

COVENANT.

CONFESSING that you have lived at enmity with your Heavenly Father, and relying henceforth upon divine grace, you do now, in the presence of God and men, solemnly choose the Lord Jehovah to be your God, the Lord Jesus Christ to be your only Saviour, the Holy Spirit to be your Sanctifier, Guide, and Comforter, the Scriptures of the Old and New Testaments to be your rule of faith and practice.

In consecration of all that you have and are to the service of God, you "join yourself (by a covenant of the Lord) into a church estate in the fellowship of the gospel, to walk in all His ways, made known, or to be made known unto you, according to your best endeavors, whatsoever it shall cost you, the Lord assisting you"; engaging, by his help, to be faithful in every personal and relative duty; to live a prayerful, earnest Christian life, aiming always to promote the interest of our Saviour's cause; to hold communion with this church in all Christian ordinances, walking with and watching over its members in love; to submit to the discipline of Christ in his house, and to its regular administration in this church; and to seek in all things its peace and welfare so long as your connection with it shall continue.

This you profess, and promise, in the strength of your Lord and Saviour, to perform.

[The ordinance of baptism here administered when requisite, after which the members of the church will rise.]

I, then, in the presence of God and these witnesses, and in the name of the Lord Jesus Christ, do pronounce you a member of this church; and we engage to treat you as such, to watch over you in love, praying the God of all grace to keep both you and us in his holy covenant, and to receive us at length into the communion of the Church in Heaven; through Jesus Christ our Saviour. Amen.

GOVERNMENT.

THE Church of the Pilgrimage is, according to its history from the beginning, a Congregational church, maintaining the polity for which its original members suffered, and in adherence to which they came to America. It recognizes all ecclesiastical power to be vested in the congregation of Christian believers, united in covenant in the local church; claiming the right to administer its own affairs according to its understanding of the Word of God, independently of all outward authority or control. At the same time it recognizes the principle of the Fellowship of the Churches as exercised in councils, in the transfer of members, in fraternal intercourse and mutual watch and care, according to the law of Christ and established Congregational usages.

In the general administration of its affairs, it observes the usual methods of Congregational churches, as laid down in the leading treatises on Congregational church government. For convenience, however, it adopts, for its more special guidance, the rules which follow.

I. OFFICERS.

The officers of this church shall be a Pastor or Pastors, Deacons, Scribe, and Treasurer, who shall be chosen by its members, by ballot, to perform respectively the duties usually appertaining to these offices. The Pastor shall be a member of the church. There shall also be a Standing Committee, consisting of the Pastor and Deacons, and as many others as the interests of the church may be thought to require, whose duty it shall be to examine applicants for admission to the church, and exercise a watchful care of its interests, and a general supervision of its discipline. The added members of this committee shall, with the Scribe and Treasurer, be chosen annually.

II. DEVOTIONAL MEETINGS.

1. A prayer meeting, unless giving place to some other religious service, shall be held on Sabbath evening.

2. A regular meeting for prayer and conference shall be held on Thursday evening, subject only to such transfer to other evenings as occasional circumstances may require. On the Thursday evening preceding the communion Sabbath, this meeting shall take the form of a lecture or some other service, preparatory to the observance of that ordinance.

3. There shall also be held on the last Friday evening of every month, except in those instances in which that evening may not directly precede the communion Sabbath, when it shall be held a week later, a church conference meeting, for the purpose of promoting Christian fellowship and acquaintance, and mutual growth in grace.

III. BUSINESS MEETINGS.

1. The Pastor of the church shall be its standing moderator.

2. It shall be the privilege of all members of the church to attend its meetings for business; but those only shall be entitled to vote who shall have attained the legal age.

3. The vote of a majority of those present and voting shall be sufficient, in the transaction of the regular business of the church. But no person who shall have received a letter of dismission from this church shall be entitled to vote upon the business before it, except upon return of the letter.

4. The annual meeting of the church for the choice of officers, and the transaction of such other business as may be required, shall be held on the Monday evening next preceding the first Sabbath in January.

5. A business meeting may be called at any time when, in the judgment of the Pastor or Deacons, it may be desirable, or at the request of five members; and any meeting, for business of special importance, shall be notified in such way and time as to allow a general attendance.

6. All meetings for business, except such as may be held at the close of a regular service, shall be opened with prayer.

IV. MEETING OF STANDING COMMITTEE.

A meeting of the Standing Committee shall be held on some evening of the third week preceding the communion Sabbath, or, in special cases, later than this, for the purpose of examining in Christian experience such persons as may desire to unite by profession with the church, or for attending to any other matters that may concern its welfare. The regular meeting of this committee shall be notified from the pulpit.

V. THE LORD'S SUPPER.

The Lord's Supper shall be celebrated on the first Sabbath of every alternate month, beginning with the first Sabbath in January.

VI. ADMISSION OF MEMBERS.

1. Persons may be admitted to this church, from other evangelical churches, by letter or certificate, presented within one year of time of issue, giving assurance of their consistent standing in the churches from which they come.

2. Persons wishing to unite with this church upon profession of faith will be expected to confer with the Standing Committee, at the meeting appointed for this purpose, and to give satisfactory evidence of personal piety. If approved by the committee, they shall be publicly propounded, unless in extraordinary cases, two weeks. The question of their admission shall be decided by vote at a meeting of the church; and, at the time of reception, they will be expected publicly to assent to its Creed and Covenant.

VII. DISMISSION OF MEMBERS.

A blank certificate shall be appended to all letters of dismission issued by this church, to be filled and returned to us by the clerk of the church to which the person shall have been dismissed and received ; and no letter of dismission given shall be valid for a longer period than one year.

VIII. TRANSFER OF CHURCH RELATION.

1. All absent members of this church, not wishing to transfer their relation to some other evangelical church, within one year from the time of their removal, will be expected to assign suitable reasons for the delay, and to renew such reasons annually so long as their membership with us shall continue.

2. Members of other churches, wishing to commune with us for a longer period than one year, will be expected to transfer their relation to us, or to give satisfactory reasons for their delay.

IX. DISCIPLINE.

The discipline of this church shall be administered according to the general principles laid down in Matthew xviii. 15 – 17.

1. In private offences when only one individual is concerned, and in private offences between two or more when neither of the two may commence labor with the other, it becomes the duty of any brother who may be especially cognizant of, or aggrieved by, the case, to commence the proper steps of discipline by a fraternal private conference with the offender. Should this prove ineffectual, the interview should be repeated with one or two others. This again failing, the matter shall be brought to the notice of the Standing Committee, who, if still unable to effect a reconciliation, shall

present it formally before the church ; and the church, if entertaining the complaint, shall, by summoning the offender to appear at an appointed time for a hearing of the case, or in such other way as may seem advisable, confer and labor with him still further, with a view to restoration ; and shall then administer the form of discipline, if any, which the case may be thought to demand.

Should the preliminary steps of labor not be taken by any brother, it shall be the duty of the Standing Committee to proceed with them.

2. In cases of open and notorious offence on the part of a member of the church, the same general course shall be pursued, with the difference only, that it shall devolve upon the Standing Committee to proceed with the required process of discipline, without waiting for a formal private complaint.

3. In case of a violation of the Articles of Faith, and Covenant, such as a change of belief, or neglect of religious ordinances, the first step taken shall consist in the most fraternal, kindly labor with the individual by the Pastor or some specially interested brother, in the hope that he may be restored ; to be followed, if needful, by the regular process. The first steps having been taken, the case shall be referred to the Standing Committee, and the order of procedure from this point shall be as in offences of the first class; no case being brought publicly before the church until the preliminary steps have been taken without avail.

4. No act of censure shall be passed, except by the concurrent vote of two thirds of the members present and voting.

X. EXPENSES TO COUNCILS.

The necessary expenses of the Pastor and delegates from this church to Ecclesiastical Councils shall be paid from the treasury of the church.

XI. RELIGIOUS CHARITIES.

1. A contribution shall be taken in connection with every observance of the Lord's Supper, for the purpose of meeting the incidental expenses of the church.

2. It shall be the duty of the church, at the annual meeting, to determine the plan of benevolence for the ensuing year, specifying the objects in behalf of which contributions or subscriptions shall be taken ; while for objects not thus specified collections may be taken, whenever, in the judgment of the Pastor and Deacons, it may be expedient.

XII. REVISION.

No alteration shall be made in the foregoing rules, unless at a meeting of the church previously notified for this purpose, and by vote of two thirds of the members present and voting. This rule shall not, however, be so construed as to forbid the temporary suspension of any rule, when the church shall see fit unanimously so to order.

OFFICERS.

(See pages 26, 27.)

PASTORS.

1. JOHN ROBINSON . . . Installed, 1609.
2. RALPH SMITH . . . . " 1629.
3. JOHN REYNER . . . . " 1636.
4. JOHN COTTON . . . . " June 30, 1669.
5. EPHRAIM LITTLE . . . " Oct. 4, 1699.
6. NATHANIEL LEONARD . . . " July 29, 1724.
7. CHANDLER ROBBINS . . . " Jan. 30, 1760.
8. ADONIRAM JUDSON . . . " May 12, 1802.
9. WILLIAM T. TORREY . . " Jan. 1, 1818.
10. FREDERIC FREEMAN . . . " Nov. 3, 1824.
11. THOMAS BOUTELLE . . . " May 21, 1834.
12. ROBERT B. HALL . . . . " Aug. 23, 1837.
13. CHARLES S. PORTER . . . " May 21, 1845.
14. JOSEPH B. JOHNSON . . . " Jan. 4, 1855.
15. NATHANIEL B. BLANCHARD . Acting Pastor, June, 1857.
16. PHINEAS C. HEADLEY . . . " " Oct., 1861.
17. WILLIAM W. WOODWORTH . " " July, 1862.
18. DAVID BREMNER . . . . Installed, Nov. 10, 1864.
19. GEORGE A. TEWKSBURY . . " April 13, 1870.

I

RULING ELDERS.

1. WILLIAM BREWSTER   .   .   .   Chosen, 1609.
2. THOMAS CUSHMAN .   .   .   .   "   April 6, 1649.
3. THOMAS FAUNCE .   .   .   .   "   " 1699.

DEACONS.

1. —— ——   .   .   .   .   Chosen, 1609.
2. JOHN CARVER   .   .   .   "   "
3. SAMUEL FULLER   .   .   .   "   "
4. RICHARD MASTERTON .   .   .   "   1626.
5. THOMAS BLOSSOM   .   .   .   "   "
6. JOHN DOANE .   .   .   .   "   1634.
7. WILLIAM PADDY   '.   .   .   "   "
8. JOHN COOK   .   .   .   .   "   "
9. JOHN DUNHAM .   .   .   .   "   "
10. ROBERT FINNEY .   .   .   .   "   Aug. 1, 1669.
11. EPHRAIM MORTON   .   .   .   "   "   "
12. THOMAS FAUNCE .   .   .   .   "   Dec. 19, 1686.
13. GEORGE MORTON   .   .   .   "   March 25, 1694.
14. NATHANIEL WOOD   .   .   .   "   "   "
15. THOMAS CLARK .   .   .   .   "   "   "
16. JOHN FOSTER   .   .   .   "   April, 1716.
17. JOHN ATWOOD .   .   .   .   "   "   "
18. HAVILAND TORREY   .   .   .   "   Jan. 22, 1727.
19 THOMAS CLARK .   .   .   .   "   "   "
20. THOMAS FOSTER   .   .   .   "   May 2, 1745.
21. JOSEPH BARTLETT   .   .   .   "   "   "
22. JOHN TORREY   .   .   .   "   Oct. 3, 1754.
23 WILLIAM CROMBIE .   .   .   "   Jan. 8, 1777.
24. JONATHAN DIMAN .   .   .   .   "   May 25, 1784.
25. EPHRAIM SPOONER .   .   .   "   "   "

26. JOHN BISHOP . . . . Chosen, Oct. 1, 1801.
27. SOLOMON CHURCHILL . . " Aug. 25, 1802.
28. LOT HARLOW . . . . " " "
29 JOSIAH DIMAN . . . . " 1818.
30. EZRA COLLIER . . . . " Feb. 21, 1828.
31. THOMAS ATWOOD . . . " April 22, 1829.
32. ANDREW MACKIE . . . . " " "
33. JOSIAH ROBBINS . . . " . Feb. 16, 1831.
34. ASA THOMAS . . . . . " 1832.
35. JESSE HARLOW . . . . " "
36. TIMOTHY GORDON . . . " Feb. 6, 1839.
37. DAVID HARLOW . . . " " "
38. JESSE HARLOW . . . . " April 27, 1859.
39. GEORGE G. DYER . . . " July 19, 1865.

PRES.ENT MEMBERS.

(See pages 2S, 29.)

No.	Name.	Mode and Date of Reception.
1.	Betsey B. Robbins,	Profession, Jan. 4, 1S27.
2.	Eunice Churchill,	1st Ch., Plymouth, June 3, 1827.
3.	Hannah Holmes,	Profession, Aug. 3. 182S.
4.	Betsey Bacon,	' May 8, 1831.
5.	Eliza J. Bartlett,	" " "
6.	Sarah Jenkins,	" " "
7.	Lucy A. Bishop,	" " "
8.	Elizabeth R. Wood,	" " "
9.	Harriet N. Robbins,	" " "
10.	Leander Lovell,	" June 19, 1831.
11.	Mercy B. Lovell,	" " "
12.	Ellis Holmes,	" " "
13.	Mary A. Faunce,	" Dec. 5, 1831.
14.	Mary R. Whitten,	" Feb. 26, 1832.
15.	Pella M. Robbins,	" Nov. 7, 1835.
16.	Sarah P. Alderson,	" Nov. 5, 1837.
17.	Patience C. Dunham,	" March 4, 183S.
18.	Sarah H. Rich,	" May 6, 1838.
19.	Timothy Gordon,	1st Ch., Weymouth, July 1, 1838.
20.	Jane B. Gordon,	" " " :
21.	Jesse Harlow,	Profession, July 1, 1838.
22.	Emily W. Hart,	Robinson Ch., Plymouth, Nov. 4, 1838.
23.	Lydia R. Nye,	Profession, Jan. 6, 1839.
24.	Abby W. Bartlett,	" Nov. 1, 1840.
25.	William Sears,	" July 4, 1841.

No.	Name.	Mode and Date of Reception.
26.	Catherine Holmes,	Profession, May 7, 1843.
27.	Hannah G. Holmes,	" " "
28.	Deborah W. Perkins,	" " "
29.	Sarah Thomas,	" June 25, 1843.
30.	Joseph A. Dunham,	" Sept. 3, 1843.
31.	Lewis Perry,	Robinson Ch., Plymouth, July 6, 1845.
32.	Mary A. Finney,	" " " "
33.	Emily Holmes,	" " " "
34.	Lydia Ripley,	" " Sept. 14, 1845.
35.	Eunice Bradford,	Cong. Ch., Plympton, Sept. 14, 1845.
36.	Rhoda Davie,	Robinson Ch., Plymouth, Nov. 2, 1845.
37.	Lucy Cornish,	Cong. Ch., Freetown, Jan. 3, 1847.
38.	Mary Jane Robbins,	Profession, Jan. 3, 1847.
39.	Lucy Loring,	Cong. Ch., Plympton, May 13, 1849.
40.	Benjamin Whiting,	Profession, Jan. 6, 1850.
41.	Maria D. Chapin,	Winnisimmet Ch., Chelsea, May 5, 1850.
42.	Elisha J. Merriam,	Cong. Ch., Mason, N. H., Sept. 1, 1850.
43.	Lucy R. Merriam,	" " " "
44.	William Morey,	Robinson Ch., Plymouth, Oct. 19, 1851.
45.	Thomas M. Paty,	" " " "
46.	John F. Hoyt,	" " " "
47.	Bethia S. Hoyt,	" " " "
48.	Betsey Hoyt,	" " " "
49.	Betsey Holmes,	" " " "
50.	Susan S. Weston,	" " " "
51.	Sarah C. Paty,	" " " "
52.	Lucy Thomas,	" " " "
53.	Lydia Bagnell,	" " " "
54.	Hannah Davie,	" " " "
55.	Mary E. Paty,	4th Ch , Plymouth, March 7, 1852.
56.	Harriet Hoyt,	" " " "
57.	Mary A. B. Dyer,	Profession, Nov. 7, 1852.
58.	Sarah T. B. Sampson,	" " "
59.	Hannah B. White,	" " "
60.	Louisa H. Sears,	" Jan 2, 1853.
61.	Edward Bartlett,	" May 1, 1853.
62.	Betsey Bartlett,	" " "

5

No.	Name.	Mode and Date of Reception.
63.	Samuel Nelson,	Profession, May 1, 1853.
64.	Eliza A. Nelson,	" " "
65.	Lucy C. Barnes,	" Sept. 4, 1853.
66.	Lucy N. Hathaway,	" " "
67.	Mercy A. Davie,	" " "
68.	Sarah W. Barnes,	" " "
69.	Sarah F. Harlow,	" " "
70.	Samuel N. Diman,	" " "
71.	Ephraim T. Paty,	" " "
72.	Catherine Morton,	" " "
73.	Mary E. Harlow,	" " "
74.	Bathsheba J. Weston,	" " "
75.	Jane G. Bartlett,	" " "
76.	Nancy F. Morse,	Robinson Ch., Plymouth, Sept. 4, 1853.
77.	Mercy B. Davie,	" " " "
78.	Hannah L. McMahon,	" " " "
79.	Lydia T. Rogers,	" " Jan. 22, 1854.
80.	Nancy E. Dunham,	Profession, Jan. 22, 1854.
81.	Prince Doten,	Central Ch., Boston, May 6, 1855.
82.	Ann E. Doten,	" " " "
83.	Harvey Weston,	Profession, July 1, 1855.
84.	Sylvanus H. Churchill,	" " "
85.	Lucretia A. Churchill,	" " "
86.	George B. Churchill,	" " "
87.	William S. Holmes,	" " "
88.	Abraham Whitten,	" " "
89.	Ruth Whitten,	" " "
90.	Sophia Finney,	" " "
91.	Mary A. Bartlett,	" " "
92.	Lydia Doten,	" " "
93.	Adeline F. Chandler,	" " "
94.	Mary J. Thomas,	" " "
95.	Susan F. Thomas,	" " "
96.	Marcia T. Hubbard,	" " "
97.	Harriet N. Gore,	" " "
98.	Deborah J. Briggs,	" " "
99.	Catherine C. Martin,	" " "

No.	Name.	Mode and Date of Reception.
100.	Susan E. Paty,	Profession, July 1, 1855.
101.	Martha Holmes,	" " "
102.	Sarah E. Wood,	" " "
103.	Charlotte W. Perkins,	Cong. Ch., Norwich, Ct., July 1, 1855.
104.	David L. Harlow,	Profession, Nov. 4, 1855.
105.	Allen Holmes,	" " "
106.	Hannah T. Holmes,	" " "
107.	Mehetabel Holmes,	" " "
108.	Susan A. Mason,	" " "
109.	Charles Whitten, Jr.,	" " "
110.	Jacob W. Southard,	" " "
111.	Nancy Robbins,	" " "
112.	Lucy Dillard,	" " "
113.	Maria S. Diman,	" " "
114.	Sarah R. Finney,	" " "
115.	Chauncy M. Howard,	Cong. Ch., Thetford, Vt., Nov. 4, 1855.
116.	Ebenezer Davie,	Profession, May 4, 1856.
117.	Lucy Marcy,	" " "
118.	Betsey Eddy,	Robinson Ch., Plymouth, July 3, 1856.
119.	Betsey T. Morton,	" " " "
120.	Lucy Harlow,	" " " "
121.	Mary L. Harlow,	Profession, July 6, 1856.
122.	Gideon Perkins,	" July 4, 1858.
123.	Joseph Kingsley,	" " "
124.	Fanny Davie,	" " "
125.	Elizabeth Fuller,	" " "
126.	Susan D. Edes,	" " "
127.	Leonice Churchill,	" " "
128.	Harriet N. Nightingale,	" " "
129.	Lucy W. Wood,	" " "
130.	Mary F. Wood,	" " "
131.	Alice S. Bradford,	" " "
132.	Clara B. Churchill,	" " "
133.	Mercy A. Sears,	John St. Ch., Lowell, Dec. 1, 1859.
134.	George F. Andrews,	High St. Ch., Providence, May 3, 1860.
135.	Adrianna J. Andrews,	Wesleyan Ch., Duxbury, May 3, 1860.
136.	George G. Dyer,	Cong. Ch., Abington, May 4, 1862.

No.	Name.	Mode and Date of Reception.
137.	Charles T. Holmes,	2d Ch., Plymouth, July 10, 1862.
138.	Margaret H. Holmes,	Profession, July 13, 1862.
139.	Elizabeth A. Holmes,	" " "
140.	Edward Hathaway,	" " "
141.	Stephen Lucas,	" " "
142.	William Bishop,	" " "
143.	Catherine B. Bishop,	" " "
144.	Susan Collingwood,	" " "
145.	Martha B. Atwood,	" " "
146.	Harriet M. Merriam,	" " "
147.	Rebecca W. Robbins,	" " "
148.	Rebecca Holmes,	" " "
149.	Caroline C. Paty,	" " "
150.	Emma Davie,	" " "
151.	Winslow S Holmes,	" " "
152.	Mary E. Holmes,	" " "
153.	Hannah J. Thomas,	" " "
154.	Ruth W. Damon,	" " "
155.	Betsey H. Josselyn,	" " "
156.	Ruth F. Burgess,	" " "
157.	Annetta Washburn,	" " "
158.	Abby R. Perkins,	" " "
159.	Mary E. Carpenter,	" " "
160.	Samuel Cole,	" " "
161.	Samuel O. Whitmore,	" " "
162.	Harvey Bartlett,	" " "
163.	Louisa F. Sears,	" " "
164.	Louisa T. Cornish,	" " "
165.	Lydia G. Nye,	" " "
166.	Cordelia A. Jackson,	Cong. Ch., Wayland, Sept. 4, 1862.
167.	Alexander Jackson,	Profession, Sept. 7, 1862.
168.	John H. Harlow,	" " "
169.	John Eddy,	" " "
170.	Angeline Dunham,	" " "
171.	Mary E. Bartlett,	" " "
172.	Ann E. Harlow,	" " "
173.	Lucy Harlow,	" " "

No.	Name.	Mode and Date of Reception
174.	Lucy A. Johnson,	Profession, Sept. 7, 1862.
175.	William A. Perkins,	" " "
176.	Priscilla P. Sherman,	" Nov. 2, 1862.
177.	Priscilla Hedge,	" " "
178.	Eliza N. Hathaway,	" " "
179.	Abby Robbins,	" " "
180.	John Eddy, Jr.,	" " "
181	Sarah Manter,	1st Ch., Ipswich, Jan. 4, 1863.
182.	Betsey D. Hall,	Profession, March 1, 1863.
183.	Mary Fuller,	" " "
184.	Sarah A. Waldron,	" " "
185.	Annie E. Churchill,	" " "
186.	Barnabas Hedge,	" " "
187.	Isaac Lanman,	" " "
188.	Lucy M. Arthur,	E St. Ch., South Boston, April 30, 1863.
189.	Judith G. Diman,	Profession, Jan. 1, 1865
190.	Sarah S. Pierce,	" July 2, 1865.
191.	Edward L. Robbins,	" " "
192.	Edward Baker,	" March 4, 1866.
193.	Sophia B. Baker,	" " "
194.	Ellen Carland,	" " "
195.	Martha H. Holmes,	" " "
196	Lucy M. Loring,	" " "
197.	Joanna B. Ellis,	M. E. Ch., Plymouth, May 3, 1866.
198.	Mary Harvey,	Profession, May 6, 1866.
199.	M. Augusta Robbins,	" " "
200.	Clarissa Bullard,	Evan. Ch., Westboro', July 1, 1866.
201.	Lizzie P. Calloway,	Profession, Jan. 6, 1867.
202.	Mary H. Clark,	Cong. Ch., Lawrence, Feb. 29, 1867.
203.	Lucy Westgate,	Profession, March 3, 1867.
204.	Mary Cornish,	" " "
205	Minnie C. Bradley,	" " "
206.	Nancy L. Pratt,	Cong. Ch., Carver, March 3, 1867.
207.	Caroline E. Peckham,	Cong. Ch., Lawrence, May 2, 1867.
208.	Nancy M. Hoyt,	Profession, July 7, 1867.
209.	Eliza Ross,	Pres.Ch., Highlands, N.Y., Oct. 31, 1867.
210.	Helena C. Ellis,	Profession, Jan. 5, 1868.

No.	Name.	Mode and Date of Reception.
211.	Mary E. Holmes,	Profession, March 1, 1868.
212.	Harriet Burgess,	" " "
213.	Josephine I. Peckham,	" " "
214.	Ellen Congdon,	Old South Ch., Boston, April 30, 1868.
215.	Levi P. Morton,	Profession, May 3, 1868.
216.	Augusta M. Morton,	" " "
217.	Helen L. Shaw,	" " "
218.	Eliab Wood,	" " "
219.	Phebe T. Wood,	" " "
220.	Francis Howland,	" " "
221.	John T. Doten,	" " "
222.	Charles H. Cobb,	" " "
223.	Prince Manter,	" " "
224.	Harriet E. Wood,	" " "
225.	Lydia A. Jenks,	" " "
226.	Ruth S. Thomas,	" " "
227.	Thomas B. Sears,	" July 5, 1868.
228.	Betsey H. Morton,	" " "
229.	Harriet B. Whitten,	" " "
230.	Abby H. Whiting,	" " "
231.	Mary F. Cobb,	" " "
232.	Lucy E. Cobb,	" " "
233.	Julia F. Sears,	" " "
234.	Mary L. Loring,	" " "
235.	James Cameron,	Pacific Ch., N. Bedford, April 10, 1870.
236.	George A. Tewksbury,	W. Cong. Ch., Portland, April 28, 1870.
237.	Curtis C. Howard,	Berkeley St. Ch., Boston, June 27, 1870.
238.	Roxanna H. Howard,	" " " "
239.	Emily B. Richmond,	Mt. Vernon Ch., Boston, June 27, 1870.
240.	Ichabod S. Holmes,	" " " "
241.	Tabitha Holmes,	" " " "
242.	Mary W. Kingman,	Union Ch., Weymouth, June 27, 1870.
243.	Albert T. Finney,	Profession, July 3, 1870.
244.	Phebe Bartlett,	Cong. Ch., Bristol, R. I., Sept. 1, 1870.
245.	Elizabeth A. Sears,	Profession, Sept. 4, 1870.
246.	William T. Paty,	" " "
247.	George W. Paty,	" " "

No.	Name.	Mode and Date of Reception.
248	Thomas A. Wallace,	Profession, Sept. 4, 1870.
249.	Harriet B. Holmes,	" Nov. 6, 1870.
250.	Mary A. Robbins,	" " "
251.	Abby H. Weston,	Berkeley St. Ch., Boston, Mar. 2, 1871.
252.	Pella W. Finney,	Mayflower Ch., St. Louis, Mar. 2, 1871.
253.	Louisa S. Jackson,	Profession, March 5, 1871.
254.	Mary B. Bradford,	" " "
255.	Rebecca Bacon,	" May 7, 1871.

THE LORD OUR GOD BE WITH US, AS HE WAS WITH OUR FATHERS. — The Prayer of Solomon.